To: Chandra
From: Karen Wood
Dec '95

THE
RAJAH's RICE

The
Rajah's Rice

Adapted by David Barry

Illustrated by Donna Perrone

A Mathematical Folktale from India

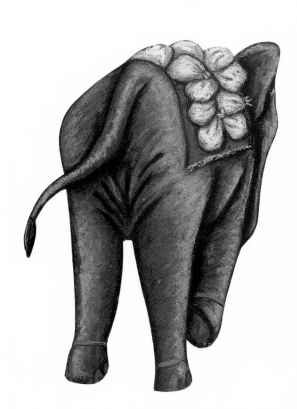

Scientific American

BOOKS FOR YOUNG READERS

W. H. FREEMAN AND COMPANY / NEW YORK

To my wife, Camilla. DB
To my family for all your love, support, and encouragement. DP

Thanks to Hezi Shoshani at the Elephant Research Foundation,
Bloomfield Hills, Michigan, and to Renée Dinnerstein and her
colleagues at P.S. 321, Brooklyn, New York.

Text copyright © 1994 by David Barry
Art copyright © 1994 by Donna Perrone
Designed by Debora Smith

Scientific American Books for Young Readers is an imprint of
W. H. Freeman and Company, 41 Madison Avenue, New York, New York 10010

Library of Congress Cataloging-in-Publication Data

Barry, David, 1949-
The Rajah's rice / David Barry.
p. cm.
Summary: When Chandra, the official bather of the Rajah's elephants, saves them
from serious illness, she exacts from the Rajah a reward more costly than he realizes.
ISBN 0-7167-6568-3
[1. Elephants—Fiction. 2. India—Fiction. 3. Mathematics—Fiction.] I. Title.
PZ7.B276Raj 1994   94-16087
[E]—dc20   CIP
                                                                        AC

Printed in the United States of America
10 9 8 7 6 5 4 3 2 1

Once upon a time a long time ago, a girl named Chandra lived in a small village in India. Chandra loved elephants. She also loved numbers. So of course she loved all numbers to do with elephants: two tusks to polish on each elephant, eighteen toenails to clean, a hundred scrubs on a side at each bath. Chandra had many chances to think about elephant numbers because she had a special job: She was the bather of the Rajah's elephants.

Chandra liked other numbers, too. As she walked past rice paddies, muddy after the harvest, she counted the snowy egrets that flew above her.

She passed through the marketplace at the edge of the village and stopped to help the spice peddler count change.

When she joined her friends where they stood watching the Rajah's elephants parade through the town square, she remembered every elephant number she knew. Then she started thinking about rice.

It was rent collection day, and bags bulging with rice hung from the sides of the elephants.

No wonder the people looked sad. The Rajah had taken so much rice for himself that the whole village would be hungry.

But this was the way it had always been. For thousands of years the villagers had farmed the Rajah's land. For thousands of years, he had come with his elephants to take most of the rice harvest.

The whole thing made Chandra angry, but what could she do?

On the elephants' next bath day, Chandra packed up her equipment and walked over the fields to the palace. She was about to enter the gates when the guard stopped her.

"You cannot come in this morning, Elephant Bather. The elephants have taken sick."

Chandra peered through the bamboo gate into the elephant yard. There she could see her elephants lying on the ground as still as felled trees. No amount of calling, singing, or cooing made them so much as raise their heads.

Over the days that followed Chandra sat watch over her precious elephants. She was not allowed inside, so she waited at the gate, watching medical men from all across the land come to cure the elephants.

The first doctor sat on cushions in the courtyard and feasted: he ate eight meat pastries, ten chickpea dumplings, and twelve sand lobsters served on banana leaves at each meal. While he ate, the elephants got sicker.

Another doctor spent all day and most of the night in the elephant yard chanting and burning incense. The elephants got even sicker.

Seven more doctors came and went, but the elephants got still sicker.

One morning, the Rajah returned from a walk in the gardens to find Chandra at the gate, staring in at the elephants. "What are you doing here, Elephant Bather?" he asked.

"I worry about the elephants," she said. "I love them all and know them well. Maybe I can help them."

The Rajah thought for a moment. "Go ahead and try," he said. "I need those elephants. Without them, I will not be able to carry the rice to market on market day. If you can save them, you may choose your own reward."

The guard opened the gates, and Chandra and the Rajah walked in silence to the elephant yard. Chandra approached Misha, the Rajah's favorite elephant. She studied his feet: the nails, the pads, the cuticles. She studied his tusks and the eight molars deep inside his mouth. She studied the lips, the tongue and the throat. She looked deep into his eyes.

When Chandra got to the first ear, she discovered a painful-looking infection inside the ear canal. The other ear was the same. So were the ears of the other elephants. Chandra cleaned their ears, sang the elephants a soothing song, and went home.

At dawn the next day, when Chandra returned, the elephants were walking unsteadily around their yard. They greeted her with joyful trumpeting.

The Rajah was overjoyed. He declared a festival day and invited everyone in the land to the palace.

The Rajah led Chandra to the ceremony room. Piled on a long table, next to the Rajah's chessboard, was a glittering array of gold necklaces, brilliant sapphires and rubies, diamond brooches, bags of gold rupees, and other treasures.

The guests began to arrive, and soon the ceremony room was crowded with villagers.

"Name your reward, Elephant Bather," said the Rajah.

Chandra looked at the beautiful jewels on the table before her. She thought about her elephants and the hundreds of sacks of rice they carried away from the village each year. And then she noticed the chessboard.

"The villagers are hungry, Rajah," she began. "All I ask for is rice. If Your Majesty pleases, place two grains of rice on the first square of this chessboard. Place four grains on the second square, eight on the next, and so on, doubling each pile of rice till the last square."

The villagers shook their heads sadly at Chandra's choice.

The Rajah was secretly delighted. A few piles of rice would certainly be far cheaper than his precious jewelry. "Honor her request," he boomed to his servants.

Two servants brought out a small bowl of rice and carefully placed two grains of rice on the first square of the board. They placed four grains on the second square. Then eight on the third square, sixteen on the fourth square, thirty-two on the fifth square, sixty-four on the sixth square, 128 on the seventh square, and finally 256 grains of rice on the eighth square at the end of the row.

Several servants snickered at Chandra's foolishness, for although the 256 grains filled the eighth square completely, they amounted to only a single teaspoon of rice.

At the first square of the second row, the servants stood awkwardly, not knowing how to count out the rice. The next number was 512, but that was too high to count quickly, and besides, it was too many grains of rice to fit on one square of the chessboard.

Chandra started to explain, "Since you had one teaspoon of rice at the end of the first row, why not just put two teaspoons—"

But the Rajah cut in. "Just keep doubling the rice," he ordered. "You don't need to count every grain."

So the servants put two teaspoons of rice into a bowl for the first square of the second row. For the second square, they put four teaspoons of rice in the bowl. Then eight teaspoons of rice for the third square, and so continued, doubling the number of teaspoons each square.

The eighth square on the second row needed
256 teaspoons of rice, which by itself filled another bowl.

On the third row, the servants started to count by
teaspoons again, but the Rajah cut in. Showing off his
knowledge of mathematics, he said, "If the sixteenth square
takes one bowl of rice, then the seventeenth square takes two
bowls of rice. You don't need to count by teaspoons anymore."

So the servants counted by bowls. Two bowlfuls for the first square, then four, then eight, then sixteen, and so on. The rice for the last square of the third row completely filled a large wheelbarrow.

Chandra's neighbors smiled at her. "Very nice," one of them said. "This would feed my family for a whole year."

As the servants worked through the fourth row, wheelbarrow by wheelbarrow, the Rajah paced back and forth, his eyes wide in amazement. His servants gathered around him. "Shall we bring rice from your royal storehouses?" they asked.

"Of course," was the reply. "A Rajah never breaks a promise." The servants took the elephants and headed out to the first storehouse to get more rice.

By late afternoon, the Rajah had collapsed onto his couch.
As his attendants fanned him with palm fronds, the servants
started on the fifth row of the chessboard, and soon they were
emptying entire storehouses into the courtyard.

Within several squares, rice poured from the windows of the palace and into the gardens beyond. By the middle of the fifth row, all of the Rajah's storehouses were empty.

He had run out of rice.

The Rajah struggled to his feet and ordered the rice to be loaded onto the elephants and taken to the village. Then he approached Chandra.

"Elephant Bather," he said to her, "I am out of rice and cannot fill the chessboard. Tell me what I can give you to be released from my vow."

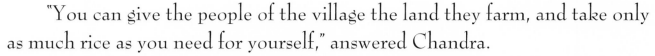

"You can give the people of the village the land they farm, and take only as much rice as you need for yourself," answered Chandra.

The Rajah gazed at the mountains of rice that filled his palace and gardens, then out beyond the gardens to the fields the villagers farmed, stretching as far as he could see. Then he looked back at Chandra, the elephant bather.

"It is done," he said.

That night the Rajah arrived in the village as Chandra and the other villagers prepared a celebration feast.

"Would you be so kind as to join me for a short walk, Chandra?" he asked. "I have a question for you."

As they strolled toward the village square, the Rajah spoke. "I am a very rich man, and it took all of the rice I owned to fill little more than one-half of the chessboard. How much rice would it have taken to fill the whole board?" he asked.

"If you had kept doubling the rice to the last square of the chessboard, all of India would be knee deep in rice," said Chandra, and smiled.

Note on the Math for Parents and Teachers

Powers of two, as mathematicians call doubling, are very powerful indeed. Taking the number 2 and doubling it 64 times (the number of squares on a chessboard) results in the number 18,446,744,073,709,551,616, enough grains of rice to fill the great volcano, Mt. Kilimanjaro.

Here is a chart that should give you a feel for how fast something will grow when you double it over and over.

Start with grains of rice.

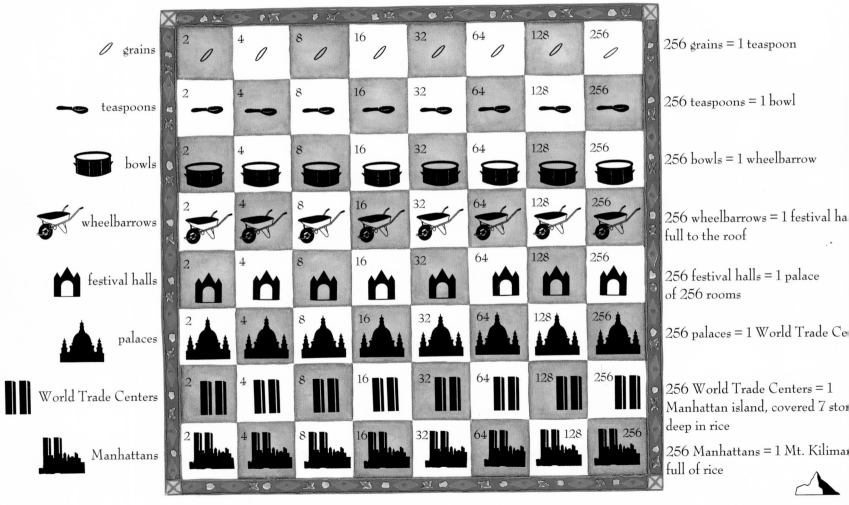

256 grains = 1 teaspoon

256 teaspoons = 1 bowl

256 bowls = 1 wheelbarrow

256 wheelbarrows = 1 festival ha full to the roof

256 festival halls = 1 palace of 256 rooms

256 palaces = 1 World Trade Ce

256 World Trade Centers = 1 Manhattan island, covered 7 stor deep in rice

256 Manhattans = 1 Mt. Kiliman full of rice

Add all 64 squares together and you get India, covered knee deep in rice.